Penguin Pandemonium

Christmas Crackers

Read more  books!

www.awesomeanimalsbooks.com

Penguin Pandemonium
Christmas Crackers

Jeanne Willis

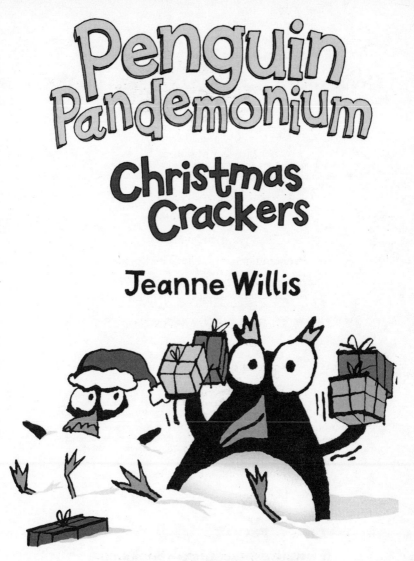

Illustrated by Nathan Reed

HarperCollins *Children's Books*

For Kelly and Dan. Happy Christmas xx

First published in Great Britain by HarperCollins *Children's Books* 2013
HarperCollins *Children's Books* is a division of HarperCollins*Publishers* Ltd,
77-85 Fulham Palace Road, Hammersmith, London W6 8JB

Visit us on the web at
www.harpercollins.co.uk

1

Penguin Pandemonium
Text copyright © Jeanne Willis 2013
Inside illustrations copyright © Nathan Reed 2013
Cover illustration copyright © Ed Vere 2013
Jeanne Willis asserts the moral right to be identified as the author of this work.

ISBN 978-0-00-752194-4
Printed and bound in England by
Clays Ltd, St Ives plc

Meet the Penguins!

Rory, Eddie & Clive

ROCKHOPPER

Looks: Rockhoppers have spiky yellow and black feathers on their heads that look like long eyebrows.

How big? 45 to 58 cm – about half the size of adult Emperor Penguins.

Favourite food: Shrimps.

Penguin party trick: Rockhopper Penguins love to burst from the water and land on the rocks with a belly flop.

Flipper fact: They hop from rock to rock, keeping both feet together, and can jump up to one and a half metres.

Little Blue, Muriel, Hatty & Brenda

Looks: Fairy Penguins have blue feathers on their heads and backs, but have white bellies.

How big? 30 to 33 cm – the world's smallest penguin.

Favourite food: Sardines and anchovies.

Penguin party trick: In the wild, Fairy Penguins are nocturnal so they only go on land at night (well past the Rockhoppers' bedtime).

Flipper fact: The world's smallest penguin – they are also known as the Little Penguin, or the Little Blue Penguin.

Paulie, Alaskadabra, Oo-Chi & Ku-Chi (chicks)

Looks: Emperor Penguins have black backs, white tummies and bright splashes of yellow and orange on their front and their ears. The chicks are fluffy and grey and their faces are white, not black.

How big?! Up to one metre tall – the world's tallest and heaviest penguin (over three times as tall as Little Blue!).

Favourite food: Squid.

Penguin party trick: When an egg is laid, the male stands with the egg on his feet to keep it warm until it hatches (this can take up to nine weeks).

Flipper fact: Emperor Penguins can stay under water for nearly twenty minutes!

Waldo, Warren & Wesley

Looks: Chinstrap Penguins get their name from the small black band that runs under their chin.

How big? Up to 68 cm (twice as tall as Fairy Penguins).

Favourite food: Little shrimps called krill.

Penguin party trick: Chinstraps are also known as Stonecracker Penguins because their call is so harsh it sounds like it could break stones.

Flipper fact: Chinstraps are the most common type of penguin – there are about thirteen million of them in the world.

Flighty Almighty

… Ahem, he's a GOOSE!

In the Bleak Midwinter

It was almost Christmas and when the penguins woke at City Zoo, their enclosure looked like a winter wonderland. The snow was so thick it had drifted against Rory the rockhopper's hutch door and he was struggling to open it. Luckily his best friend, Blue, the fairy penguin, was passing by when she heard his cry for help.

"What's up, Rory? Are you stuck?" she called.

"No, I'm just yelling for fun… Of *course* I'm stuck!" he wailed. "There seems to be something really heavy wedged against my door, like an elephant."

"There was a record fall in the night," said Blue.

Rory stopped yelling for a moment. "Of elephants?"

"Of *snow*, silly," said Blue, trying to brush it away with her flippers. "It's no good, I can't shift it. I'll have to go and borrow a shovel from Waldo. Wait there, Rory."

"Like I'm going anywhere," he sighed.

Blue waddled off as fast as she could in the direction of the chinstrap penguins. Waldo had a large collection of lost property that visitors had left at the zoo and, among the hats, spectacles, trolleys and trinkets, there were some tools that the workmen had left behind. There was bound to be something she could use to dig Rory out.

She had only got as far as Big Paulie's Palace when she stumbled across Waldo and his friends, the Arty Party Penguins. They were trying to clear snow away from Paulie the boss's front step. Unfortunately there was no shovel, so they had to make do with a trowel and a pogo stick that

Wesley and Warren took turns on, jumping up and down to break the ice.

"That's the way, boys!" said Waldo. "Imagine you're astride a pneumatic drill."

He waved cheerily at Paulie. The mighty emperor penguin was pacing up and down behind the palace window with his baby niece and nephew, Oo-Chi and Ku-chi, hanging off his flippers.

"Don't worry, sir, we'll soon have you out!" shouted Waldo.

"Dig faster!" mouthed Big Paulie. "These kids are doing my head in."

Blue smiled. Paulie was the best boss the penguins could ever have. He'd been in charge since the day he arrived from the Antarctic and they all feared and respected him – all except for the emperor chicks, who never gave him a moment's peace.

"Unky Pooey, uth wanth to go out-thide *now!*" squealed Oo-Chi.

"Me ith going to make a big fat thnowball," cheeped Ku-Chi.

Just then, Warren did an extra hard bounce on the pogo stick, a big chunk of ice fell away from the door and, to Paulie's great relief, he was free. His immediate concern was for the other penguins – were any of them trapped inside their hutches?

"We freed the fairy penguins earlier," said Wesley. "We could hear Muriel screeching from the other side of the pool."

"Rory is still trapped," said Blue.

Waldo picked up his trowel. "I can't

bear to think of that sweet boy missing his breakfast squid," he frowned. "Lead on, Miss Blue. Arty Party Penguins to the rescue!"

But, by the time they'd staggered back, Rory was waiting for them outside with his rockhopper mates, Eddie and Clive.

"Hey, Blue," he grinned, "what took you so long?"

Blue looked around. There was no sign of a spade. "How did you escape, Rory?"

"Brolly power," he said.

Eddie and Clive had managed to dig him out with the pointy end of an umbrella that they'd borrowed from the brown bears who overlooked the penguin pool. As usual, the bears insisted on taking all the credit.

"If it hadn't been for our umbrella, Rory would have missed lunch as well as breakfast," growled Orson.

"I hope the spokes aren't damaged," added Ursie. "We need it for our dance routine. We've come up with a new one for Christmas and it goes like this: a-one, two, three, four…"

He grabbed Orson by the paw, did a ridiculously high kick – and fell over on the ice, pulling the other bear on top of him.

"Honestly, you two. Get married!" cackled a familiar voice.

It was Muriel with the two faithful members of her girly gang, Hatty and Brenda. The bears leapt up and brushed themselves off.

Waldo put his flippers on his hips and looked Muriel up and down. "You shouldn't tease them," he said. "It's the season of goodwill. If the bears want to hug each other, that's lovely."

"We were *not* hugging!" insisted Orson, waving his paws in the air. "We were just dancing and we slipped."

"Yeah, right. I know a hug when I see one," chortled Muriel, tapping her beak. "And I know another secret, don't I, Hatty and Brenda? Go on, tell Rory and Bloop!"

Hatty and Brenda shuffled nervously. They weren't sure of the answer and, if they got it wrong, there was a good chance that Muriel would shout at them.

She tapped her webbed toes impatiently and glared at them. "Hatty and Brenda, tell Bloop and Rory our secret!"

"That you're in love with Warren?" blurted Hatty.

"And you think he's cuddly?" added Brenda.

Muriel blushed and put her head under her flipper.

"No, I'm not! No, I don't!" she fibbed as Warren sidled off and hid behind a bush. "I meant the *other* secret… about Santa's Grotty."

Blue looked at her sideways. "What's…
a grotty?"

"She means Santa's *Grotto*," said Brenda,
waving a leaflet about *Christmas at City
Zoo* that had blown into the penguin pool.
"Someone has built a funny shed thing
near our enclosure – there's a photo of it
here, see?"

She tapped the leaflet and Rory peered
at it quizzically. "When did this happen?"

"The builders were banging about
all morning," interrupted Ursie. "You
wouldn't have heard it because you were
snowbound in your hutch, but we can see
it all from here."

"If you don't believe us, have a peek
through your viewing grille," said Orson.

All the penguins waddled over, pressed their beaks to the little opening in the wall of their enclosure and gazed in amazement at the wooden chalet covered in fairy lights.

"So sparkly!" sighed Hatty.

"So twinkly!" twittered Brenda.

"So what's it for?" asked Blue.

"Ask Miss Brainstorm," said Muriel, clapping her flippers to get Brenda's attention. "Brenda, you like showing off your reading skills. Tell Bloop what it says about Santa's Grotty in that leaflet."

"It's *Grotto*," said Hatty.

"Like *you* can spell," snorted Muriel.

Brenda cleared her beak and used the tip of it to follow the words. "It says that someone called Santa is coming here."

"Who's Santa?" asked Blue. "Do you know, Rory?"

Before Rory could answer, Ursie's paw shot up. "Ooh… I know, I know! He's a chubby bloke with a long white beard. When we were cubs, we spent Christmas at the zookeeper's house and we saw him, didn't we, Orson?"

Orson put his chin in his paws and thought back. "Ah yes, happy days," he sighed. "The smell of the turkey... the Christmas tree... the kids hanging up their stockings on Christmas Eve. If they were good, Santa brought them presents— Lordy, here he comes now! He's in the penguin enclosure!"

Muriel whisked round and saw a portly figure trudging towards them through the snow. "*Santa!*" she squealed. "I've been a good penguin. Give me a present!"

But it wasn't Santa, it was Big Paulie.

"Do I look like a fat guy with facial hair?" he grunted.

It was an easy mistake to make in the dim winter light. Paulie was the biggest penguin in the pool and he was carrying the chicks, so, from a distance, their fluffy feathers looked like a white beard.

Blue gave a small sigh. "Oh. I really hoped it was *You Know Who*, didn't you, Rory?" she whispered.

Rory nodded. "Yeah. Oh well, maybe Santa will come next year."

Big Paulie shook his beak and frowned. "Don't get your hopes up, my little friend. Santa never visits the likes of us."

Muriel pulled a face and stamped her foot in the snow. "*Why not?* I want a

Christmas present!" she sulked.

Big Paulie held out his flippers and did his best to explain. "Muriel, the giving of gifts is a *human* tradition. Every Christmas, Santa comes all the way from the North Pole to visit City Zoo to give out presents, but they're just for the children, not the animals."

"That is *tho mean*, Unky Pooey!" squealed Oo-Chi, tweaking her uncle's head feathers.

"Unky Pooey, why doethn't Thanta like penguinth?" wailed Ku-Chi. "Why-why-why?"

Big Paulie counted patiently to ten and put the chicks down. "I don't make the Christmas rules— *Ouch!*"

"Ha ha! Got you in the botty with a
thnowball!" shrieked Oo-Chi.

Trying to keep his dignity, Paulie shook
one leg, then the other, to shake the ice off

his tail, and almost slipped. Rory grabbed him by the flippers to steady him.

"I'm fine," insisted Paulie. "Just practising the snow dance Orson taught me."

"I recognised it straight away," said Rory, trying not to laugh. "Paulie, can I ask you something?"

The emperor penguin regained his balance. "As long as it's not personal. I'm a very private penguin. Whaddya want to know?"

"It's about Santa," said Rory.

Paulie let out a long groan. "Santa *again* already?"

Paulie clearly wasn't in the best of moods and Rory was just beginning to think that maybe he should stop asking questions, when Blue butted in.

"We just want to know why we've never seen Santa's Grotto before if he comes here every year," she blurted. "Don't we, Rory?"

Paulie waved a dismissive flipper. "It's usually over by the reindeer paddock," he said, whisking round as one of the chicks crept up behind him. "No! Don't do you dare throw that snowball at me, Ku-Chi— *Ow!* That's it! I'm taking you back to your mother!"

He grabbed the chicks and turned to go, when Muriel kicked off again.

"It's not fair! We want presents, don't we, Hatty and Brenda?"

"We want bobble hats!" said Brenda.

"We want hamsters!" said Hatty.

Even Rory got caught up in the excitement. He only wanted a small gift, but to a penguin who lived to do stunts, it would be a dream come true.

"And I'd really like a set of sparkly wheels for my skateboard!" he whooped.

Paulie looked over his shoulder and fixed him with his beady eyes. "We're penguins," he said as he waddled away, "and penguins do not celebrate Christmas."

"We'll see about that!" muttered Muriel.

CHAPTER TWO

Jingle Bells

Despite the fact that penguins weren't supposed to celebrate Christmas, they were very excited when Santa arrived at City Zoo in his sleigh. He had a sack full of presents in the back and the brown bears were certain he might have brought a little something for them.

"He's here!" hollered Ursie. "Let's show him our stockings – we might be in luck."

"I don't wear stockings," growled Orson. "Keep your voice down."

The penguins rushed over to the grille.

"Look at the reindeer," remarked Clive.

"Rain, dear?" repeated Eddie. "I thought it was snow. Ursie, can I borrow your brolly?"

There was a long queue of children leading up to the grotto and, as Santa parked himself in a rocking chair, the first little girl went over and sat on his lap.

"And what would you like for Christmas, young lady?" he asked.

"A giraffe, please."

Santa gave a small groan, fished about in his sack and gave her a thin, square parcel.

"It looks a bit flat for a giraffe, doesn't it, Clive?" mumbled Eddie.

"That's because it's a colouring book," said Clive, who was more interested in the elves. "Who are those little green dudes in the funny hats and curly shoes?"

Brenda looked it up in her leaflet about *Christmas at City Zoo*.

"They're Santa's little—"

"Aliens!" shouted Orson.

"Helpers!" said Brenda.

Ursie was confused.

"Santa's little alien helpers? That's just weird."

"That's Christmas for you," said Orson.

But while everyone else was getting into the festive spirit, Muriel was getting angrier by the minute.

"Oh my cod!" she wailed. "Why is he giving those naughty kids presents and not us? Brenda, get a pencil and write a letter to Santa for me! OK, I want: bubble bath, leg warmers, pink fluffy mules…"

"Eek – got no pencil!" said Brenda anxiously.

"Um – got no paper," said Hatty.

Rory grabbed his snowboard. "Muriel, you're a penguin. Penguins don't get presents, remember?" he said. "Come on, Blue, let's show the visitors our crazy moves."

Blue hesitated for a moment, mesmerised by the tinsel on the Christmas tree, then she went off with Rory and the rockhoppers to entertain the crowds with their daring stunts.

Having warmed up with a few beak-bonks against the enclosure wall and some impressive rodeo-flips off the diving board, Rory gathered his crew together.

"We've got a nice big audience," he said, flipping his board with one foot. "Let's wow them with a new twist on the tail-wheelie."

"Like what?" said Clive.

"Like whoa!" said Eddie.

Rory jumped on his snowboard and raced over to the fake mountains. Where the snow had fallen on the rocks, it had created a set of steep steps – perfect for bouncing down from a great height.

"What we could do, which would be really exciting…" he began, but Blue had already read his mind and was halfway up the mountain.

"Yay! Tail-wheelies into staircase-jumps, right, Rory?"

"Right, Blue."

Rory stepped aside and, as the crowd gasped at the speed and courage of the little blue fairy penguin bouncing perilously from ledge to ledge, Rory knew it was a brilliant move.

The next morning, Rory was woken at dawn by a loud rap on his hutch door. He yawned, got out of his nest and went to see who it was. He thought it might be Blue, but it wasn't.

"Sorry to disturb you so early, dear boy," said Waldo, "only, my pogo stick has gone missing. I wondered if you might have borrowed it."

Rory shook his head. "Where did you leave it, Waldo?"

"Outside Paulie's Palace," he winced. "I asked if he'd taken it inside to have a little bounce, but he said no and told me to go away, very loudly. He was *ever so* grumpy."

Paulie could be quite fierce at times – especially first thing in the morning; he wasn't an early bird.

"I expect he just got out of the wrong side of the nest, Waldo," said Rory. "Come on, I'll help you look for your pogo stick. I bet the chicks have hidden it as a prank."

But they hadn't. Rory and Waldo had only got as far as the frozen pool when Ursie waved at them frantically from the tree in the bear paddock.

"Yoo hoo! There's been a kerfuffle! Muriel's gone over the top!"

Rory sighed. The bears were terrible stirrers. They were always spreading rumours, and nine times out of ten, they weren't true.

"Muriel's gone over the top of what?"

"The wall!" said Ursie. "I'm not even lying."

Rory wasn't so sure. "How on earth could she get over the wall on her own?"

Rory had been over the top a few times himself. It wasn't too difficult if he formed a pyramid with the others, but it was far too high for a fairy penguin to climb on her own.

"But that's just it – she wasn't on her own. She was with Hatty and Brenda," said Ursie, climbing down from the tree. "Back me up, Orson!"

Orson lumbered over to the barrier and leant over.

"They all bounced over together," he

said, "on a pogo stick. *Boing, boing...*
wheee!"

Waldo clapped his flippers over his beak.
"Boing, boing, wheee?"

"Actually, it was boing, boing, *boing,*
wheee," added Ursie. "There were three
boings and a whee. Orson can't count,
which explains his bad dancing."

As far as Rory was concerned, it didn't
matter how many boings there were. More
to the point, where had Muriel and the
girls gone – and why?

"Blue wasn't with them, was she?" he
asked.

"I'm here!" called Blue, skidding across
the snow towards him. "Come quickly,
Rory! Muriel's done something really silly.

We have to get her back before the zoo opens."

She grabbed his flipper and they hurried over to the wall of the enclosure. The pogo stick lay in the snow where it had fallen.

"Where's Muriel gone?" panted Rory.

Blue ran over to the viewing grille and pointed towards the grotto. "Look – there she is!"

Rory's beak fell open. "I don't believe it!"

Muriel was sitting in Santa's sleigh with Brenda and Hatty, opening the presents in the sack.

"Nope, this one's a toy soldier... don't want that. Ooh, mittens!"

"Muriel!" yelled Blue. "*What* are you doing?"

Muriel whisked round and waved at her. "I'm doing Christmas! I've got all sorts of lovely presents: mittens, muffs— Oh, here's something for you, Bloop. It's bubble bath. Believe me, you need it."

"*Muriel*, you have to get out of there now!" said Rory. "The zoo's about to open. If you get caught, goodness knows what the keeper will do with you, let alone Paulie!"

Muriel took no notice, tore off another piece of wrapping paper and held up the contents. "Christmas underpants! I might give these to Warren. Any requests, Rory?"

"Yes!" he wailed. "Get back in the

penguin enclosure. You'll get Hatty and Brenda into big trouble."

But Muriel didn't seem to care. "Go jingle some bells, Rory," she said. "*Tis the season to be jolly.* Sing up, girls!"

"*Fa la la la la…*" hummed Hatty.

"*… la la la la,*" sang Brenda.

They were having such fun Rory couldn't help feeling a bit left out. For all he knew, there might be some sparkly wheels in Santa's sack. Surely it wouldn't hurt just to nip over the wall for a few minutes and have a rummage? But if he said it outright, he would look greedy, so he took Blue to one side and made up a good excuse.

"We have to go and get the fairy penguins

back," he said. "I should hate them to get into trouble. Especially at Christmas."

But, as usual, Blue saw straight through him. "Dear Rory," she grinned. "You're always thinking of others. And while you're saving Muriel, you can see if there's a present you might like."

"That never even crossed my mind," he said innocently.

Blue smiled a knowing smile.

"OK, I admit it," said Rory, "I would like to open something. Wouldn't you?"

Blue knew she'd been rumbled. It would be lovely to undo the shiny ribbons and see what was inside those beautifully wrapped parcels.

"I'll fetch the pogo stick," she said.

There was a flat rock near the wall. The snow had already been brushed away by certain fairy flippers to create a good surface to bounce off, so Rory picked up the pogo stick and held it steady.

"On you get, Blue. I'll put my feet either side of yours, then, on the count of three, we bounce."

They held on to the pole.

"We'll do six boings, let go of the stick and land on the wall," he said, putting his flippers round her. "One, two, three… Bounce harder, Blue!" urged Rory. "That's it – four, five, six… Now let go!"

She almost missed the wall and, if it hadn't been for Rory, she might have fallen back into the enclosure, but she

was so light,
he was able
to pull her up.

"You OK,
Blue?"

"Fine!" she
said. "Don't
fuss; I'm not
a girly. I'm
not *Muriel*."

She leapt fearlessly off the wall and
landed neatly in the thick snow, unlike
Rory, who went into an undignified skid
and did a backwards roll. Blue stuffed
both flippers in her beak to stop herself
snorting, but a giggle escaped.

"I'm not laughing at you, I promise,"

she said, helping him up as the tears rolled down her cheeks.

Rory brushed himself down and scowled at her. "What are you laughing at then?"

"*Tis the season to be jolly!*" sang Blue as they ran to the sleigh. "Ho ho ho!"

But she soon stopped laughing. Out of the corner of her eye, she spotted someone dressed in red striding towards the grotto – a man with a long white beard and snowy whiskers, leading a reindeer with very impressive antlers.

"Santa's coming!" she squealed. "Everybody hide!"

There was only one place for five little penguins to hide on a sleigh – in Santa's sack. They all dived in, pulled the gifts on top of them and held their breath.

"Easy, Rudolph," said Santa. "Stand still while I harness you up, there's a good lad."

The penguins could hear the reindeer pawing the ground and the jingle of bells as Santa took hold of the reins. "Trot on, Rudolph," he said. "Away we go!"

Blue felt a sudden jolt and was thrown against Rory. "Eek! The sleigh's moving!" she panicked. "Quick, we have to get off!"

"Yes! Yes, we do," said Rory. "That's what I was thinking."

But it was too late.

"Oh my cod!" screamed Muriel. "We're gathering speed. Rory, *do something!*"

But there was nothing Rory or any of them could do and, as Orson and Ursie looked on in disbelief, the sleigh disappeared out of the zoo gates.

CHAPTER THREE

Santa Claus is Coming to Town

If Santa had taken his eyes off the road and looked over his shoulder, he would have seen his sack wriggling like mad. It was stuffy and dark in there until Rory pecked some holes in it so they could see out.

Despite being squashed between four fairy penguins, a train set and a doll that said "Mama!" whenever the sleigh hit a bump, Rory was enjoying the ride enormously. He'd never been out in the big, wide world before and the sight of all the cars, houses and shops was all very new and exciting.

Muriel, however, did not like it at all. Every time they went round a corner, she screamed. If it hadn't been for the roar of the traffic, Santa would have heard her.

"Shush!" said Blue. "You've got us into enough trouble already."

Muriel pulled a face and retched. "I don't care!" she said. "I feel sleigh-sick! Hatty, give me your hat to barf in."

Reluctantly, Hatty handed over the woolly hat she'd borrowed from the talking doll and gave it to Muriel.

"*Mama!*" said the doll.

"Shut up; don't talk to me," snapped Muriel. "I'm ill."

If Blue was feeling nervous, she hid it well. Like Rory, she had never left the zoo before and had no idea where they were. She peered through the holes in the sack at the snow-covered city and frowned.

"Rory, is this the wild? Is it the Antarctic, where Big Paulie was born?"

Rory had no idea, but he was determined to find out and, when Santa stopped at a red traffic light, he undid the drawstring and poked his head out of the top of the sack.

"Brenda, see that sign with the picture of two old people on it? What does it say?" he asked.

Brenda stood on top of Hatty's head to get some height, and spelt out the letters.

"E-l-d-e-r-ly C-r-o-s-s-i-n-g."

"So *that's* where we are," said Rory. "We're in Elderly Crossing, Blue."

They weren't, of course. It was simply a warning sign for drivers to slow down near the Sunny Glades Retirement Home, but he wasn't to know that. The lights turned green and, as the sleigh set off again, Rory got back in the sack and pulled the drawstring tight.

"I wonder where we'll end up," he said.

"I wonder how we'll get home," sighed Blue.

She was a plucky little penguin, but she felt safe in the penguin enclosure and she was worried that she would never see the inside of her hutch ever again.

"It will be all right, Blue. I'll look after you," said Rory reassuringly.

"Oh, please. Now I feel really sick," gagged Muriel. "Brenda, hold the hat open."

Just when they all thought the journey would never end, the sleigh took a sharp right, went through a set of iron gates and parked under a bike shed. The penguins watched through the sack as Santa tethered the reindeer and made his way towards a large building.

"Where's he going?" said Muriel. "Brenda, stop gibbering; get out of the sack and read what it says on the gates," she commanded.

Brenda crawled out, rubbed her eyes with her flippers and tried to decipher the lettering. "It says, 'Welcome to Wheatfield's Infant School'; what's a school?"

Nobody knew, but just then some children arrived down the front path, lots of children, all whooping and shouting. The penguins ducked down in the sleigh, out of sight. They watched as the infants threw snowballs and made skid runs and built snowmen.

The penguins weren't exactly scared – they saw children every day at City Zoo, after all. But there had always been a barrier between them. These children, however, were noisy, boisterous – and on the loose. Goodness knows what they would do if they spotted five penguins in the playground. It didn't bear thinking about.

A teacher came out of the building and rang a hand bell and the children lined up and went inside. There were hundreds of them, all dressed in the same red uniforms with winter coats over the top.

"I don't think much of their fashion sense," muttered Muriel, preening her feathers. "Blue is a much prettier colour. Red is so *yesterday*."

Rory waited until the last child had gone in, and then hopped out of the sleigh.

"Let's sneak inside," he said. "I want to know what a school is."

It was a reckless thing to do, but Blue was up for it. There was no turning back and, even if it ended in disaster, at least it would be an adventure – something to tell her grandchicks when she was old.

"Maybe it's a zoo for kids," she suggested. "That building is probably their enclosure."

"They must have been born in the wild, judging by the way they behave," sneered Muriel. "They remind me of monkeys. Do they remind you of monkeys, Hatty and Brenda?"

"Gibbons," said Hatty, "only not as hairy."

"Baboons," added Brenda, "only not as clever."

Keeping their heads down, the penguins crept up to the school entrance. Making sure the coast was clear, they stepped inside and found themselves in a cloakroom. Hanging on the pegs were lots of small hats, scarves and coats, which would make perfect disguises.

"Look at me! I'm a schoolgirl!" said Brenda, trying on a blazer. "Ooh, there's something in the pocket."

"It's a sandywich!" exclaimed Hatty, pulling on a pair of Wellingtons.

Muriel snatched it from her. "Is it squid? *Eughh*, it's stinky yellow stuff!" Muriel, like the rest of the penguins, had only ever eaten seafood and fish at the zoo, and the taste of cheese and pickle came as a nasty

shock to her. She spat it out through the holes in the fluffy scarf she'd wrapped round her face.

"*Bleugh! That sucks!*"

Suddenly the door opposite the cloakroom opened. To their dismay, a teacher came marching out of the school hall with a line of children behind her. She took one look at the penguins and, mistaking them for pupils, wagged her finger at them.

"What are *you* doing here? You were meant to be in assembly. If you want to see Santa, I suggest you get in line now and follow Class One into the playground – *quietly!*"

The penguins did as they were told. Caught up in the occasion, they trooped outside with the children and followed the teacher over to the sleigh where Santa was waiting.

"Who would like to be one of Santa's little helpers?" asked the teacher.

Muriel's flipper shot up immediately.

"Put it down!" said Blue. "You'll give us away."

It was too late. Seeing Muriel with her penguin features hidden by the scarf and coat, the teacher mistook her for a well-behaved child, and chose her.

"You're standing nice and sensibly," she said. "Unlike the rest of Class One! Choose some friends to help, then go and give out the presents with Santa."

Muriel made a big performance of choosing her friends. She picked Hatty and Brenda, but hesitated when she got to Rory and Blue.

"Hmm. I think you two have been *rather bad*," she mumbled through her scarf. "I'm not sure how much help you will be to Santa."

"Stop messing about," whispered Rory.

Muriel tutted and pointed a mittened flipper at the two of them.

"Good, off you go, you five. Stand by the reindeer – he won't bite you," said the teacher.

"Will Santa bite us?" asked a small girl.

The teacher shook her head. "No, Charlotte. Of course Santa won't bite."

"Why not?" she said. "Hasn't he got any teeth, miss?"

Before the teacher could stop her, she climbed on to Santa's lap and checked.

"He's got plastic teeth. Santa, are you my grandad?"

The teacher stepped in and removed her before she snapped the elastic on his beard. "Charlotte Higginbottom, let go of Santa.

And if anyone else decides to make a silly remark, we will *all* go back inside!"

Santa adjusted his whiskers and gave the penguins some more presents to hand out to the waiting children. Each infant felt the gift carefully and gave it a squeeze and a shake. Not knowing what was inside made it even more exciting, and their faces shone with happiness.

"I think giving is even more fun than getting, don't you, Rory?" said Blue.

"It makes me go all tingly," he agreed as a tiny girl flung her arms round his neck and gave him a thank-you kiss.

But Muriel wasn't feeling the tingle at all and was refusing to hand the gifts over. "Mine, I think!" she said, hiding another gaily wrapped package inside her coat.

Unfortunately Blue spotted her and wasn't about to let her get away with it.

"Give it back, Muriel."

Muriel gazed at her blankly. "Give what back, Bloop? I never took anything, did I, Hatty and Brenda?"

"No," said Hatty, "except for the present in your coat."

"And the one under your hat," added Brenda. "And the one down your boot."

Rory gave Muriel a hard stare. "Give them to the children… or I'll frisk you," he warned.

Muriel ground her beak and glared at him for a second, then she backed down.

"Honestly, can't you take a joke? I was only playing," she muttered, feeling under her hat and revealing a little box covered in shiny foil. The smallest boy in the class held out his hand hopefully. Forgetting that she was meant to be a human, Muriel gave it to him in her beak.

"There!" she said. "Happy Christmas, you lucky, lucky little man."

The boy couldn't understand a word of bird language, but even so, he had a funny feeling that Muriel was no elf.

"It's a penguin, miss!" he beamed. "I love penguins, I do. Mister Santa, please can I have a penguin for Christmas?"

"Don't be silly, Damian," said the teacher, "you can't have a penguin for Christmas. You already have a present. Now move along, dear."

Muriel did a little victory dance. "I am the mistress of disguise!" she hooted. "If that teacher thinks I'm human, maybe I can fool Santa too and he'll put something in my stocking."

"Dream on, Muriel," sighed Blue. "Nobody can fool Santa."

"No," said Rory, "but we all fooled the teacher. You know what this means?"

Blue shook her head.

"It means that we can go into her classroom disguised as kids and see how they celebrate Christmas!" said Rory, punching the air triumphantly with his woolly mittens.

So when Santa went to the staffroom for a tea break, that's exactly what they did.

CHAPTER FOUR

We Wish You a Merry Christmas

After the thrill of seeing Santa, Class One took a while to calm down and the teacher was beginning to regret letting them loose with pots of glue and glitter. It was time for their art and craft lesson and, as it was almost the end of term, they were making decorations and Christmas cards.

"From what I can see, they're just making a mess," snorted Muriel.

Unbeknown to anybody in the classroom, there were five penguins hiding in the Wendy house over by the book corner. They'd crept in while the children had gone to wash their hands after petting the reindeer, and had been watching the activities through the plastic window for some time now.

"Now, Damian," said the teacher, "what's that you're painting, dear?"

The child held it up proudly. "A spaceman, miss."

The teacher blinked hard. "That's not

very Christmassy, is it? Why don't you draw a nice robin?"

"OK," he said, sucking his crayon, "I'll draw a nice alien robin in a space rocket."

There were six children round each table, all of whom were doing different things. While Green Table were busy making cardboard angels and sticking cotton wool up their noses, Red Table were trying to strangle each other with pretty paper chains.

Over on Yellow Table, a little girl with glitter in her eyebrows had painted a fairy penguin in a fluffy scarf. Muriel recognised it instantly – it was a picture of her.

"Oh my cod, Hatty and Brenda. Look, I'm a work of art!"

To her annoyance, she wasn't the only one. The other children had also drawn penguins, and not just any old penguins either. They were unmistakably the same penguins who had helped Santa give out the presents. The youngsters must have seen through their disguises, but, being children, they were far too clever to think there was anything odd about them.

"Ooh, there's a drawing of *me*," whispered Brenda. "So glittery!"

"And one of me," said Hatty. "So sparkly!"

"So chubby," tutted Muriel. "I thought it was a snowman. And there's one of Bloop looking cross-eyed. Goodness, it's just like a photograph."

Blue ignored her. It was the best thing to do with Muriel because if there was one thing she hated, it was being ignored.

"Bloop!" said Muriel, poking Blue in the ribs with a crayon. "Did you hear the funny thing I just said? About you being cross-eyed?"

Blue was perfectly capable of sticking up for herself, but Rory hated it when Muriel teased her. He and Blue had been friends since they were eggs and he leapt to her defence.

"It wasn't funny, Muriel, and it's not true. Make Blue a Christmas card to say sorry."

Blue clapped her flippers together excitedly. She wasn't bothered about Muriel apologising, but making Christmas cards for each other was a great idea. When the children went out to play, the penguins would be safe to leave the Wendy house and set to work with the scissors and sequins.

"Yay! Let's make cards and send them to all the penguins we love!" she said.

"Oh, Warren," swooned Muriel, sliding on to the doll's bed in the Wendy house, "*you're* all the penguins I love."

The other penguins didn't hear exactly

what she'd mumbled in her scarf, but the name *Warren* was pretty clear.

"Why are you all grinning at me?" she scowled. "I just said that I love all the penguins – what's so funny about that?"

"I think I'll make Warren a card," said Blue playfully.

Muriel screwed up her beak. "No, you can make one for Rory," she said pointedly. "*He's* your boyfriend, poor thing, and Brenda and Hatty can make lots for me because I am their best friend."

Muriel didn't seem to understand the meaning of Christmas. Maybe it was because she was a penguin or maybe it was just because she was Muriel, but the others were really getting into the swing of things.

"Let's make a card for Frosty," said Rory. "I bet polar bears celebrate Christmas."

Frosty was a little polar-bear cub who had stayed at City Zoo for a short while last year when he'd hurt his paw. The penguins had befriended him and helped him get better, so he could go back and live with his mother in the wild. They got regular updates on him from a migrating Arctic tern called Thermal, but they missed Frosty. A Christmas card would be a lovely way to keep in touch.

"But how will we get it there?" wondered Blue. "Thermal won't be able to carry a card all the way in his beak, will he?"

As if on cue, the teacher clapped her

hands and made an announcement.

"Listen, everybody. It's nearly playtime, so leave your cards to dry in front of the radiator, then when you get back, who can remember what we're going to do next?"

Damian put his hand up. "Are we going into outer space to blast the Martians, miss?"

She shook her head. "No, dear, we are going to put our cards into envelopes, write our addresses on the front and stick stamps on. Then what are we going to do with them?"

Damian put his hand up again, but the teacher chose someone more sensible.

"Yes, Charlotte?"

"I need a wee," said Charlotte.

"So do I," squeaked Hatty. "Do you need a wee, Brenda?"

It seemed that they all did, but, like Charlotte, they would have to wait until playtime.

"Then, after play," said the teacher, "we'll post our cards in the letterbox in the hall and the postman will deliver them."

"What's Frosty's address, Rory?" whispered Blue.

"Frosty, the Arctic, in the Wild," he said. "There's only one Frosty. It'll get there."

It seemed like a good plan and when the bell went for playtime and the classroom was empty, the penguins drew the blinds and, armed with cardboard and scissors, they hurried over to Purple Table and sat down to make their cards.

If it was hard to handle scissors and glue with fingers, it was even worse with flippers. The cardboard was very stiff and the glue was a lot stickier than it looked, and they got more sequins and glitter in their feathers than on the paper.

"You have something stuck to your beak, Rory," whispered Blue. "A pink sequin."

"*Pink?*" exclaimed Rory, picking frantically at his nostrils. "Has it gone?"

Blue nodded.

"Do I have anything on my face, Rory?"

She had a bit of silver tinsel stuck to her forehead like a halo, but it looked so cute, he didn't mention it.

"You look fine," he said, accidentally

spattering himself with an overloaded paintbrush. Painting wasn't easy with beaks and for the first time in their lives, the penguins appreciated how artistic Waldo, Warren and Wesley were. The Arty Party Penguins were famous for producing pictures that nobody recognised – and now the others could see why.

"That's such an amazing card," said Hatty, looking over Muriel's shoulder. "Is it a hippopotamus in the snow?"

"No, you're looking at it upside down," tutted Muriel, turning it up the other way and holding it next to her face. "It's obvious what it is. Tell her, Brenda!"

Brenda struggled to guess. "Is it a… lovely Christmas pudding?"

Muriel sighed and looked at her pityingly. "Oh, Brenda. You might be able to read, but you know nothing about art. It's a portrait of *me*! Wesley will love it."

"It's like a photograph," said Blue, adding the finishing touches to Frosty's card. She'd already made one for Rory and the chicks and was struggling to think what to paint for Paulie.

"How about a salmon?" said Hatty. "Big Paulie likes salmon. It's his favourite."

"That's a good idea, only we haven't got any salmon-coloured paint," said Brenda.

They all racked their brains.

"A picture of me?" wondered Muriel. "I'm his favourite, after all."

"I know!" said Rory, ignoring her. "Let's paint him a snow scene of the Antarctic. It would remind him of where he grew up."

"Brilliant!" said Blue. "We can all do a bit each, then, when it's finished, we can sign it with our footprints."

Shielding the card he was making for her with both flippers, Rory shook his head.

"We can't sign it. Paulie will know we left the zoo. It has to be anonymous."

Muriel put her masterpiece in front of the radiator to dry and stomped off towards the paper cupboard. She had been admiring the colourful paper chains hanging from the classroom ceiling and decided to make something similar to decorate her hutch. Having watched Red Table making them earlier she decided that it looked easy enough. It was a simple matter of sticking lots of strips of shiny foil into circles and looping them together – so she thought – but having spilt the glue, the strips of paper seemed to have a mind of their own. When she tried to join the chain together, one of the loops got stuck round her beak.

The more she struggled to flick it off, the tighter it got. She tried to call for help, but by then the glue had dried and her beak was clamped shut.

"Muriel's very quiet," murmured Rory as Brenda helped him address Orson and Ursie's card to THE BROWN BARES, SITTY ZOO.

"Peaceful, isn't it?" said Blue.

It was only when they had returned from posting the cards in the hall that they realised something was wrong. By then,

Muriel was hysterical, but as she still had the paper chain wrapped round her beak, all she could do was wave and pull faces.

"Maybe we should leave it on," suggested Rory.

But he was only joking. Muriel might be a bossybeak, but she had rescued him that time he jumped into the lions' den to save Oo-Chi and Ku-Chi. She was a good penguin deep down so, with Blue's help, he unpeeled the loop.

Just then a teacher rang the school bell in the playground and the children marched into the dining hall. Now that her beak was free of paper chains, Muriel could smell a wonderful aroma. Something was cooking, it smelt a whole lot better than raw mackerel and she was hungry.

"Who says penguins can't have Christmas dinner?" she beamed.

"Paulie," said Rory.

But Paulie wasn't there and the penguins had left without any breakfast.

"Let's go, girls!" commanded Muriel.

CHAPTER FIVE

Bring Us Some Figgy Pudding

Rory sniffed the air and got a waft of roast potatoes and stuffing balls. Although his favourite food had always been squid, he'd never smelt anything so delicious. Adjusting his disguise, he grabbed Blue by the flipper and hurried to the dining room behind Brenda and Hatty.

Doing their best not to waddle, they tried to mingle among the children, but the clattering of dishes and chattering of children were deafening. As the infants jostled excitedly in the dinner queue, Muriel cowered behind a pillar with her flippers over her ears.

"It's like feeding time at the zoo!" she wailed. "I've seen baboons with better manners."

Rory, however, was too hungry to care and looked longingly at Charlotte Higginbottom's plate as the dinner ladies dished out her food.

"Mmm," he said, "what are those lovely slices of white stuff?"

"Any more turkey, Charlotte?" asked the dinner lady.

Turkey? Rory and Blue exchanged worried glances. There was a free-range turkey at City Zoo called Cyril who often came and chatted to them through the viewing grille. He wasn't very handsome, but he was good at telling jokes and Blue liked anyone who could make her laugh.

"Rory, I think they're eating Cyril," she gulped.

He gave her a comforting pat. "They wouldn't do that. Cyril's very old, Blue. He'd be way too tough."

Blue sighed with relief.

"We could do with another bird in the oven!" shouted the cook. "I've never known such hungry children."

The penguins stared at each other in horror.

"Another bird?" gasped Muriel. "What if the cook runs out of turkey and decides to roast us?"

"Calm down. People don't eat penguins," said Rory.

But Muriel wasn't convinced. "They might at Christmas!" she squeaked. "Hatty and Brenda have got a lot of meat on them and I'm delicious. *Let's hide!*"

Blue tugged at Rory's coat. "What if Muriel's right? People do eat very funny things."

By now, even Rory was beginning to feel a bit nervous as he watched the rows of children eating at the dining tables. Damian had already finished and was going back for seconds.

"We will run out of turkey at this rate!" laughed the dinner lady.

"*Run!*" said Rory, heading for a large trestle table covered in a long velvet tablecloth that was pushed against the wall. The penguins dived under it and hid.

"I don't want to be eaten, do you, Brenda?" sniffed Hatty.

"Not even a little bit," wailed Brenda.

"It's OK, we're safe now," said Rory reassuringly. "Everyone relax."

BANG! BANG, BANG, BANG, BANG! A series of small explosions went off around the room.

"Oh my cod, we're under attack!" panicked Muriel.

"We can't be," said Rory. "The kids are all laughing and joking."

He lifted the edge of the tablecloth slightly and peered out.

The children were pulling their Christmas crackers.

"Look!" he whispered. "It's nothing to be scared of."

One by one, the penguins peeked out and watched as the kids played with their cracker toys, put on their tissue-paper crowns and read out the corny jokes.

"Damian, why did the chicken cross the road?" asked Charlotte.

"Coz there were no cars coming," he said, poking her with a little toy Martian.

"No," pouted Charlotte, "that's not the answer."

Rory dropped the tablecloth back down, leant back and smiled.

"I know why the chicken crossed the road – to get to the other side! Cyril told me."

"I don't suppose Cyril celebrates Christmas," sighed Blue. "His relatives get eaten."

Maybe Cyril didn't know that. He wasn't born in a barn – he'd hatched at City Zoo like she had and he knew very little about the outside world.

"I think it's best if we don't mention roast turkeys to Cyril," advised Rory. "But we could collect some of the cracker jokes for him. He'd like those."

Suddenly the room was plunged into darkness.

"Arghhh! It's the end of the world!" shrieked Muriel.

But it wasn't. The headmistress had just closed the curtains and turned off the lights. A sudden hush fell over the dining hall.

"I don't like it," said Blue. "It's too quiet. What's happening?"

Rory lifted the end of the tablecloth again. The cook was striding across the room carrying what appeared to be a steaming ball of black sponge decorated with a piece of holly.

"That looks a bit prickly to eat," he remarked.

"What does?" muttered Blue, poking her head out.

"Ooh!" squealed the children. "It's the Christmas pudding!"

Muriel cheered up immediately. "Pudding? Hatty, your head's in the way. Let me see the pudding!"

The penguins watched as the headmistress took a box of matches out of her pocket, lit one and hovered it over the top of the pudding. To their disbelief, it was in flames.

"Fire!" yelled Rory. "The pudding's on fire!"

Forgetting that he was supposed to be hiding, he was about to run out from under the table when Blue caught him by the tail and pulled him back under.

"*Shush!* Come back, Rory!"

"No, go back out there!" said Muriel. "Throw a jug of water over it, Rory. I don't want a burnt bit."

"The children are clapping and cheering," said Brenda in a puzzled tone. "Maybe people always set fire to their Christmas puddings."

Muriel looked at her as if she was mad. "Why would anyone do that?"

"Perhaps it makes it taste even better," said Hatty. "I'll let you know."

By now, the pudding had gone out and,

as the lights came back on, the children tucked happily into their dessert.

"I will never understand people as long as I live," muttered Rory. "Whatever will they do next?"

Right on cue, the headmistress stood up and made an announcement.

"Children, you can wrap up warmly and play in the snow when you have finished your pudding," she said. "After that, you have one more lesson, then we'll put the fairy on top of the Christmas tree."

Muriel had a glint in her eye – the kind of glint she always got when she'd just had an idea.

"Fairy?" she said. "*I'm* a fairy penguin, aren't I, Brenda and Hatty? The tree is in the hall, right?"

"Don't even think about it," said Rory.

But Muriel couldn't get it out of her mind.

CHAPTER SIX

Walking in a Winter Wonderland

The penguins waited under the trestle table until all the children had gone. Then, when the canteen shutter closed and the cook and the dinner ladies were busy in the kitchen, they crept out. There was a lot of dropped food under the dining tables and the penguins were hungrier than ever.

"*Eugh!*" said Rory, sampling a stray Brussels sprout that Damian had wedged under a chair. "Give me squid any day. I'm glad I'm not human. How do they eat this muck?"

"Beats me," said Blue, spitting out a roast parsnip. "But I did like the crackers once I got used to the bangs."

She was fascinated by the little toys the children had left behind among the mess of cardboard tubes, shiny paper and abandoned jokes. There was a tiny bag of marbles, a whistle and a plastic monster. There was even a spinning top.

"It seems silly to waste them, Rory,"

she murmured.

He picked up a bracelet made from brightly coloured glass beads and elastic. "It does," he agreed. "Muriel, what have you got on your head?"

Muriel did a twirl and patted her face feathers. "It's my cracker crown," she announced. "I'm a princess, aren't I, Hatty?"

But Hatty had stuffed her beak with Christmas pudding and the answer came out wrong. "Yes, your Real Horridness," she said, battling with a bit of custard skin.

"It's Royal *Highness*," insisted Muriel, "isn't it, Brenda?"

But Brenda was busy pecking a piece of meringue shaped like a snowman and wasn't concentrating properly. "Hmm?" she said. "Real Horridness? Yes, that's right."

Muriel gave her a steely stare and, suspecting that she was about to spoil the mood, Rory quickly changed the subject and pointed out of the window.

"Look at the children! They're having a great time skidding and sliding in the playground," he said. "Who wants to go outside and have a game of snowballs?"

Everybody's flipper went up.

"Me! Me! Me!" shouted Muriel, forgetting to be cross. "But no throwing them at my tail feathers, OK? I've just preened."

"We promise," said Hatty and Brenda, waddling over to the door.

"Check your disguises, everyone," said Rory. "Muriel, I can see your tummy."

"You shouldn't be looking!" she said. "Brenda and Hatty – tuck me in! You're meant to be my wardrobe assistants. Tighten my scarf."

"Like this?" said Brenda, giving the ends a tug.

"Not *that* t*ight!*" protested Muriel. "You'll strangle me!"

"Can I help?" said Hatty.

Blue tapped her foot impatiently, which wasn't easy in Wellingtons.

"Hurry up, Muriel. The snow will have thawed by the time you've got ready."

Muriel looked her up and down. "One of us needs to make an effort, Bloop, and your gloves don't suit your hat."

True, she was wearing non-matching mittens, and her fake-fur hood kept falling over her eyes, but what did it matter? Blue threw her flippers in the air.

"Who cares what we look like, as long as we don't look like penguins!"

"Remember to walk not waddle," said

Rory, leading them outside to a quiet corner in the playground behind the sports shed. "We don't want to stand out."

They needn't have worried. The infants only had little legs and, bundled up in thick layers of woolly jumpers, hats, scarves and coats, they waddled in the snow just like penguins.

Rory bent over to make a snowball, creating a perfect target for Muriel, who immediately threw the one she had made earlier at his bottom.

"One–nil!" she beamed as he whisked round, clutching his tail.

"One all!" replied Blue, throwing a well-aimed missile at Muriel, which landed on top of her hat like a bird in a nest.

Muriel blinked in disbelief, then, grinning from ear to ear, she gave the command.

"Play-fight! Hatty and Brenda, roll faster!"

It was supposed to be Rory and Blue versus Muriel, Brenda and Hatty, but somehow, in the middle of the game, they all ended up in a giggling heap.

"Let's make snow angels!" said Blue. She'd seen some of the girls in Year One doing it earlier and, rolling on to her back, she flapped her flippers up and down to make wings. Hatty and Brenda copied her, and even Muriel – who was usually no angel – joined in and made a beautiful one.

"Come on, Rory!" encouraged Blue.

"Boys can be angels too."

But Rory's mind was elsewhere. He'd been watching Damian and Charlotte building a snowman. They had rolled a big snowball for its body, a smaller one for its head, then, using stones, a satsuma and a twig, they made it some eyes, a big orange nose and a mouth.

"See that brilliant snowy person over there, Blue?" he said. "Let's make our own. Let's make… a snow penguin!"

Muriel leapt to her feet. "Oh yes! Let's make a snow *me*! Up you get, Hatty and Brenda. Start rolling a me-sized snowball."

Rory held up his flipper. "I'm thinking we should build a snow rockhopper penguin," he said.

"It's all about you, isn't it?" said Muriel sourly. "We can't do a rockhopper, the head feathers are too sticky-up. Let's make a chinstrap penguin. They're very handsome… well, one of them is."

Blue dusted the snow off her feathers and drew a little circle in the snow.

"Why don't we make a snow Paulie?" she suggested. "He's the biggest so he'll really stand out."

Muriel thought about it for a moment. "OK," she agreed. "As long as I can make his face. I'm the best at making faces, aren't I, Hatty?"

"Yes. Yours is very funny," said Hatty, who wasn't listening properly.

Between them, the penguins scooped snow into the space that Blue had drawn and kept adding to it until the pile was the height of an emperor penguin.

"Right, let's pat it into shape with our mittens," said Rory. "Whoops, you nearly had his head off there, Brenda!"

Muriel waddled over to a holly bush to fetch some berries. "These are for his eyes," she said. "Brenda, Hatty – give me a leg-up. I can't reach to put them in."

After much deliberation, Muriel pressed two of the biggest berries on to the snow penguin's face and smiled. "Perfect!" she said. "It looks just like the real thing."

But there was something missing.

"It needs a beak," said Rory, waving a carrot that Santa's reindeer had left behind. He helped Muriel push it into position and the penguins stood back to admire their handiwork.

"Brilliant," said Blue. "Paulie would be proud."

Just then, she heard a small, child-like cough and spun round. The real penguins had been so busy making the snow penguin, they hadn't realised that they were being watched. Damian and Charlotte were standing behind them.

"Children to the rear," whispered Rory. "Nobody say a word. They might go away."

But the children had no intention of leaving. Damian squatted down and pressed his nose against Rory's beak.

"See, Charlotte – it *is* a penguin. I've always wanted a penguin!"

Charlotte bobbed down to check on Muriel.

"Hello, Mr Penguin!" she said, shaking
her by the flipper.

"I'm not a mister, I'm a *miss*!" hissed
Muriel.

But, of course, Charlotte didn't understand.

"Do you penguins want to play skidding with us?" she enquired.

"I made a really good slide," said Damian. "Come and see!"

Blue leant over to Rory and whispered in his ear. "Dare we?"

Rory was very tempted, but just as he was thinking it over, a teacher rang the bell for the end of play.

"Boo," said Charlotte, "we have to go in. Now we can't play with the penguins. Come on, Damian, we don't want to miss the Christmas fairy."

They ran off, but Damian had only gone a few metres when he slipped on the skid-run he'd made earlier and fell in a pile of brown slush.

"I'm all wet, miss!" he wailed.

The teacher hurried over and checked him for bruises. "You're fine. Up you jump," she said. "You need to change into dry clothes. Come with me and I'll find you some trousers and socks in the lost-property box."

The penguins watched as the children trooped inside.

"Come on," said Rory, "let's sneak back in."

"Yes, we don't want to miss the Christmas fairy either," said Blue. "You're really looking forward to it, aren't you, Muriel? Muriel?"

But Muriel was nowhere to be seen.

CHAPTER SEVEN

Oh, Christmas Tree

"**W**hy would Muriel sneak off like that?" said Rory. "Where can she be?"

He would never have guessed, but ever since the brown bears had mentioned that children hung up stockings on

Christmas Eve, Muriel was determined to do the same. She was desperate for a present and maybe if she wished hard enough, Santa would come. There was only one problem – she had no stocking.

So when she heard the teacher mention spare socks in the lost-property box, Muriel had followed her. She hid behind the coats in the cloakroom and waited until Damian had changed into dry clothes. As soon as he'd gone, she waddled out and rummaged through the box of lost school uniform to see if she could find a nice big sock to use as a Christmas stocking. To her delight, there were several, ranging from little ankle socks to long football socks – enough, in fact, for her and all her friends. She stuffed several into an old PE bag and made her way to the hall.

Having sorted out a stocking, she thought she'd go and look at the Christmas tree in the school hall to see the fairy penguin on top of it. There was no one in there – the children were all in class having lessons – so what harm could it possibly do?

*

"There's only one place left to look for her," sighed Rory, scratching his head.

They'd been everywhere: in the kitchen, in the girls' toilet, they even looked in the lost-property box, but Muriel wasn't in there. Not any more.

"Let's try the hall," said Blue. "She got very excited when she heard about the

Christmas fairy, didn't she?"

They tiptoed in and hid behind the piano in case a teacher came by.

"Wow!" said Rory. "The tree looks amazing."

The staff had decorated it at lunchtime and, although the fairy lights hadn't been turned on yet, it was shimmering with tinsel and ornaments. The penguins had never seen anything so beautiful and crept out to have a closer look. Blue gazed into a shiny bauble and jumped back at the sight of her warped reflection.

"Rory, is my face really that weird?"

"Yep!" he joked, pushing his face against an even bigger bauble. "Is my beak really that big?"

"Yep… and look, Rory, there's a tiny glass penguin on that branch."

She touched it gently with her flipper and watched it spin on a bright gold thread. It was an emperor penguin; she could tell because it had a golden yellow throat, just like Paulie. She wondered if he'd noticed they were missing yet. She didn't want him to worry.

"Oh, and see behind that star? There's a polar bear just like Frosty," said Rory.

Among the sprayed pine cones and chocolate coins wrapped in foil, there were lots of animal decorations, including a flock of robins on springs. Surely no one would mind if they borrowed a few?

"Careful," warned Blue as Rory tugged at the penguin decoration. "You're rocking the tree. It'll fall over."

"I'm not rocking the tree – you are!" he said.

"I'm not even touching it," insisted Blue, holding her flippers up to prove it.

They both stood back, but to their dismay, the tree was still wobbling in its pot, which was very odd because they were nowhere near it. Now it was shaking violently.

"OH… MY… COD!" wailed a voice. "I'm fall…ing! Catch me, Brenda and Hatty!"

The penguins looked up. There, clinging to the top of the Christmas tree for dear life, was Muriel with the PE bag over her shoulder.

"How did she get up there, Brenda?" whispered Hatty. "Did she fly?"

"Penguin's can't fly," said Brenda matter-of-factly. "I bet she bounced on that bouncy thing."

There were several pieces of gym equipment nearby, including a small trampoline, which looked as if someone had pushed it near the tree on purpose.

"Don't jump, Muriel!" said Rory anxiously. "You'll damage the tree."

"If I don't jump, I'll damage me!" she wailed.

Rory scanned the room and thought quickly. Maybe he could climb up one of the gym ropes and rescue her? No, not with flippers, it was too risky. But then he spotted a set of wall bars a bit like a ladder that went from the ceiling all the way down to the ground. There was a bolt in the floor to stop them moving, but if he undid it, he could swing the frame out at an angle near the tree. The rungs were quite far apart, but, with a bit of courage, a penguin could manage them.

"Blue, help me move these wall bars out," he said, undoing the bolt. "Muriel, swing your leg on to the top rung and climb down."

"Noooo!" she cried. "I'm too young to die!"

She had frozen in terror. It was clear that someone would have to fetch her or she'd be there until next Christmas.

"Rory, hold the wall bars still – I'll go," said Blue boldly.

"What shall we do?" asked Hatty and Brenda.

Blue shrugged and began to climb. "I don't know. Say soothing things to Muriel? Keep her calm."

Blue might have been the smallest penguin in City Zoo, but she was one of the bravest. It was a long way up for such a little bird, but she was fearless.

"Think happy thoughts, Muriel," called Hatty.

"Think of Warren," said Brenda. "Think how much he'll love your card with a Christmapotamus on it."

Muriel forgot where she was for a

second, let go and wagged her flipper angrily at Brenda.

"It is *not* a Christmapotamus, Brend— Aargghhhhh! Nearly slipped!"

"Hang on tight," said Blue, "I'm nearly there. What's in that bag?"

"Nothing," mumbled Muriel.

It didn't look like nothing, but this was no time to argue, and while Hatty and Brenda wondered out loud if it was a present for Warren, Blue found herself level with the top of the Christmas tree and held out her flipper.

"Hold on to me, Muriel. Just step on to the wall bars and don't look down."

Very shakily, Muriel did as she was told for once and, with Blue's help, she made it down.

"I just wanted to be the Christmas fairy penguin," she sniffed. "Why can't penguins celebrate Christma—"

"Hurry, the children are lining up outside!" said Rory. "They'll be here any minute."

"Eek, where shall we hide, Rory?" panicked Hatty, dancing up and down on the spot.

"Over there!"

They ran towards the stage. There was a life-sized Nativity scene in front of the curtains. Around a manger there were some figures made of badly painted papier-mâché: Mary and Joseph, the Three Wise Men, some shepherds in tea-towel headdresses, a cotton-wool sheep, a funny-looking cow and a wobbly donkey.

"Grab a crown off those men with beards, Rory!" said Blue. "Put it over your head. They'll think you're one of them!"

Copying Rory and Blue, Hatty and Brenda snatched a tea towel each and pretended to be shepherds. There was only one place left for Muriel to go.

"Move over, baby!" she screamed, jumping into the manger.

"Shh! Everyone keep still – the children are coming in," said Rory.

Hopefully, no one would spot them.

CHAPTER EIGHT

Away in a Manger

The music teacher sat down at the piano and, as the children came in, she played 'Away in a Manger'. It was so slow and sweet that Muriel could hardly keep her eyes open. It was warm in the hay and, although baby Jesus's foot was digging into her ribs, she began to drift off.

Rory, however, was wide awake. Damian was sitting in the front row next to Charlotte. He was wearing lost-property trousers that were too small for him and he had the fidgets. He had a good view of the stage and, as his grandma took him to church every Sunday, he knew the Christmas story back to front.

"Charlotte," he said, peering at the Nativity scene and counting the figures. "What does one plus one plus one plus one plus one plus one plus one make?"

Charlotte put her head on one side and thought about it. She was good at playing the cello, even though she hated it, but she was no good at sums, and this was rather a long one.

"Um… I think it's… Why?"

"There's only meant to be three Wise Men," said Damian, "but there's more."

"How many more?" asked Charlotte, counting on her fingers. "Is it eleventy?"

Damian shrugged. "Don't know. But that one's a penguin – and that one! And—"

"No shouting, please, Damian," said the teacher. "I know you're excited about the fairy lights, but Mrs Slingsby won't turn them on if you are noisy."

Just then, the music stopped and the headmistress came in. "Good afternoon, everybody," she said.

The children answered her with a long, drawn-out reply. "Good af-ter-noon, Mrs Slings-by. Good after...noon every... bo...deee."

The headmistress waited for them to finish. "Welcome to our Christmas assembly. Shortly, I will be turning the fairy lights on, but first I'd like to say a big thank you to Class Two for making the Nativity scene on the stage behind me. The lovely Wise Men and the lovely shepherds and the—"

"Lovely penguins!" called Damian.

Mrs Slingsby adjusted her glasses and looked at him sternly. "No calling out, Damian, or you will *not* be going to the carol concert at City Zoo tonight."

Rory's beak fell open. "I didn't know anything about a concert at the zoo!" he whispered. "Did you, Blue?"

She daren't shake her head in case the tea towel fell off, but, by the look on her face, she was as surprised as him. Blue felt a lump in her throat and it wasn't a Brussels sprout. There was going to be a wonderful Christmassy event at their own zoo and the penguins had no way of getting back. They were going to miss it. Suddenly Blue felt really sad. It had been a great day, but enough was enough.

"I want to go home, Rory," she whispered.

He did too. He missed Eddie and Clive, he even missed the brown bears and he certainly missed his dinner, but right now his best friend looked as if she was about to cry.

"We'll go home as soon as we've seen the fairy lights," he mouthed, "I promise." He had no idea how, but Blue didn't need to know that. He racked his brains as the teachers closed the blinds. It was almost dark outside. Maybe they could hide in the boot of Mrs Slingsby's car and get back to the zoo that way. But what if she only had a pushbike?

The headmistress went over to the Christmas tree and clapped her hands. "When everybody is sitting nicely, I will turn on the fairy lights."

The room fell silent.

Then Damian put his hand up. "Miss, did penguins visit the baby Jesus? Only I can hear one snoring."

The headmistress gave a sharp intake of breath. "I'll just wait until Damian stops being silly," she said. "Ready? Let's count down from five, everyone."

Those who could count backwards did

their best, and, although Charlotte got her five muddled up with her three, eventually the whole school reached number one and the Christmas tree lit up. The children and the penguins gasped with delight.

"Oooooh!"

"Wake up, Muriel," said Brenda, poking her with a shepherd's crook, "the fairy lights are on!"

The penguins gazed at them in wonder.

"Wow! They're beautiful, aren't they, Rory?" whispered Blue. But he was so overcome with the magic of it all, he couldn't speak.

"They're even more beautiful than me," sighed Muriel, peeking through the straw.

"Yes, they are!" agreed Brenda and Hatty.

The headmistress clapped her hands. "Charlotte Higginbottom will now play our first carol on the cello," she said, struggling to get the enormous stringed instrument out of its case.

"Boo," muttered Charlotte. The cello was three times bigger than her and, although her mother told everyone she loved playing it, Charlotte felt like kicking it off its stand.

"Come along, dear, don't be shy," said Mrs Slingsby kindly, helping her on to a chair so she could reach the strings. Charlotte opened her music book, grabbed her bow and, after a squeaky start that sounded as if someone had trodden on a rat, she began to play, accompanied by the piano. Encouraged by the teachers, the children began to sing.

"*Silent night, holy night…*"

Blue gave Rory a nudge. "Sing up!"

He shook his head so hard, his crown almost fell off. "I don't know the words, Blue."

"Nor do I. Just go *la la la*."

Rory threw open his beak and sang his heart out and, although he didn't sound quite human, nor did the school choir.

"*All is calm, all is bright!*" warbled the headmistress.

But Muriel was not the slightest bit calm. "Oh my cod! Tonight is Christmas Eve," she said. "I have to go home and hang my stocking or Santa won't come. Brenda, call me a taxi."

"What stocking?" asked Blue.

Before Muriel could answer, the piano teacher went into a rousing song about Santa getting stuck up a chimney and going *Atchoo, atchoo, atchoo*. As the penguins listened to the words, it became clear that this was his favourite way to deliver presents, even though the soot went up his nose and made him sneeze.

Muriel looked worried. "My hutch hasn't got a chimney! How will Santa put a present in my stocking?"

"Never mind your chimney, he won't come at all if we can't get home," sighed Blue.

The piano stopped playing and the headmistress made another announcement. "That was beautiful singing, thank you, children. We have now come to the end of our assembly."

"Hooray!" shouted Damian.

"Your parents are waiting to pick you up to take you home now," she continued. "If you're going to the carol concert at City Zoo tonight, please be back here at six o'clock on the dot. We don't want to keep the coach waiting. Charlotte, please leave your cello in my office. I'll ask the driver to load it on to the coach, then you can play it at the zoo."

"Do I have to, Miss?" said Charlotte.

"Yes, it'll be lovely," said Mrs Slingsby.

As the children filed out of the hall, class by class, Rory couldn't believe his luck.

"There's a coach," he said. "We can go back home on the coach!"

Blue threw her flippers round him. "I knew you'd think of something, Rory. Now we won't miss the concert."

"And I can hang up my stocking," said Muriel. "I'm outta here, baby Jesus."

"*What* stocking?" asked Rory, staring at her bulging PE bag.

But Muriel was in such a hurry, she fell

out of the manger and landed on a sheep, so he never did get an answer.

"Rory," wondered Blue, "how will we hide on the coach? Our disguises might work from a distance, but not if we have to sit next to the children."

"We'll hide under the seats!" he said triumphantly.

"But we have to get on to the coach first without being seen," said Blue. "How?"

Rory hadn't thought of that.

It was four o'clock. He had until six to come up with a solution. Was it long enough or would they all miss the coach?

CHAPTER NINE

Hark! The Herald Angels Sing

Now that the children and the teachers had gone home, as long as they avoided the cleaners, the penguins had the run of the school. They had two hours to kill before the coach arrived, so while Rory sat in the classroom trying to think how to get on it without being seen, Blue amused herself by drawing a snow scene on the whiteboard.

"I think we should leave a message for the children," she said. "Only I'm not very good with words. What shall I write, Rory?"

Rory looked up from the little scribbles he'd made of coaches and penguins and scratched his head. "I dunno. How about *The penguins were here?*"

"It needs to be a little bit more… Christmassy," said Blue, snapping the lid off the red whiteboard pen. "For example, we could say, *Dear Infants, Merry Christmas from the penguins at City Zoo.*"

Muriel put her feet up on the desk and

leant back casually. "We could *say* it, Bloop, but could we spell it?"

"Brenda can," said Hatty.

Blue gave her the pen. It was a great message, but it was much harder to write than it looked. There were some very long words and Brenda was struggling.

"Does Christmas begin with a curly C or a kicking K?" she wondered, sucking the end of the pen.

"Don't worry about the spelling too much. It's the thought that counts," said Blue.

Having done her best, Brenda stepped back and read it out loud.

"*Deer Infunts, Mary Cristmess from tha pengwins at Sitty Zoo.*"

The penguins gave her a little round of applause.

"Thanks, Brenda. That's brilliant," said Blue.

But Muriel had to have the last word. "Very good, but that is *not* how you spell 'zoo', Brenda. It has three O's, not two."

She was wrong, of course, but as no one else could read, and Brenda didn't want to argue, she added another 'o' for luck.

Rory looked at the clock. It was almost five and he still hadn't come up with a plan.

"I can't think of a thing," he said. "I'm really sorry."

Blue gave him an encouraging squeeze. "You'll think of something, there's still time. Charlotte's the one I feel sorry for. Fancy having to play that great big cello in front of everybody."

Rory's eyebrow feathers shot up in the

air. "That's it!" he whooped.

Blue had no idea what he was on about. "What's what?"

"The cello case! Let's take the cello out and hide in there. If we grab the bow straps under the lid, we could shut ourselves inside."

The case was big enough to hold four fairy penguins and a rockhopper with room to spare. The teacher would never know they were inside when she handed it to the driver, and he would put it on the coach and when they got to the other end and Charlotte undid it…

"She'd have no cello to play!" said Blue.

"She'll be so happy," said Rory, "and so surprised to see us, she won't believe her eyes, and we'll just run back to the penguin enclosure."

Muriel stopped colouring in the holly berries Blue had drawn on the snow scene and turned round. "It'll never work," she said.

"It has to," grinned Rory. "By the way, you need to check your make-up."

Muriel waddled over to the little mirror on the teacher's desk and shrieked. "Argh! I've got red pen all over me – I look like a parrot!

Why didn't you tell me, Hatty? Brenda, stop giggling!"

Rory knew that the cello was in the headmistress's office – she'd told Charlotte to leave it there earlier – so, as soon as Muriel had finished preening, they all set off to find it.

The office was near the entrance to the school and, as the cleaners still needed to vacuum, it was unlocked. There was no sign of the cello, but there was a walk-in cupboard at the back of the room. The penguins thought it was bound to be in there.

"Oh, barnacles, I can't open the door," said Rory.

Blue hunted around in Mrs Slingsby's

desk drawer and held up a little key. She waddled over and gave it to Rory. It fitted. He flung the door open and there was the great big case, leaning against some shelves. Between them, the penguins managed to lie it on the floor, undo the brass clips that held it shut and remove the cello.

"We'll have to hide it," said Blue. "Help me to shuffle it behind those filing cabinets."

Rory, Hatty and Brenda put their backs into it, but the instrument was really heavy and it was impossible to see where they were going, so while they pushed and Blue dragged, she guided them.

"To you... to me... back a bit... back a

bit more— *Stop!* I can't hold it!"

The cello slid sideways and fell with a splintering crash behind the cabinet, twanging its strings on the way down.

"Well done," said Muriel, poking Rory in the bottom with the cello bow. "But I'm not getting into that empty case if I can't breathe. It was bad enough in Santa's sack."

Rory tapped the cello case with his beak, but it was too tough for him to make a dent.

"You could make some holes with these scissors," said Blue, taking a pair from a stationery pot and feeling the pointy ends. "Rory, you hold the blades in position and I'll hit them with a heavy object."

"Like Hatty?" snickered Muriel.

"Like a paperweight," said Blue.

It worked. By the time they'd finished making holes, the cello case looked as if it had been attacked by woodworm, but at least they'd be able to breathe. It was quarter to six. The coach driver would arrive soon to pick up the case.

"In we get," said Rory. "Muriel, do you have to bring that PE bag?"

"Yes," she said, "it's for... *medical* reasons."

They all piled in. The bottom of the cello case was lined with silk, so it was quite comfortable, but Muriel soon found something to complain about. She was too hot in her fluffy scarf, which made her even grumpier than usual.

"Hatty, your beak is in my ear. Remove it this second!"

"It won't come off," said Hatty. "It's stuck to my face."

"*Shush*," said Rory, "I can hear footsteps!"

The penguins held their breath as the headmistress came into the office with the driver.

"It's in my walk-in cupboard—" she said. "That's funny, I'm sure I locked it."

"I expect you had a busy day and forgot," said the driver. "No harm done."

As he lifted the cello case on to a trolley, the penguins clung to the bow strap to stop the lid flying open. It was very dark inside and the holes were too small to see through, but they could feel themselves being wheeled across the office carpet, down the corridor and out into the playground across the gritty snow. A car hooted in the distance.

"We must be on the pavement, near the road," whispered Rory.

They could hear children and grown-ups chatting, then they felt the case tip as the trolley wheels went up a ramp and on to the coach.

"Is that my cello?" said a little voice.

"Yes, Charlotte," said Mrs Slingsby, "the driver is putting it in the luggage hold. We don't want it to get damaged, do we?"

"I do," muttered Charlotte. "I hope it falls over and breaks into matchsticks."

Finally, all the passengers were on board

and, when Damian had stopped drawing on the windows, the engine started. Blue sighed with relief. "We're off, Rory! We're going home."

As it wasn't being pulled by a reluctant reindeer, the coach trip back to City Zoo was much quicker than the sleigh ride to school. This was just as well because, although there were air holes in the case, Rory had wind after eating his Brussels sprout and it was getting very unpleasant in there.

"Was that one of Brenda's or is there a skunk in here?" groaned Muriel, clutching her beak.

"Wasn't me," said Brenda indignantly.

"Or me," said Hatty. "Must have been

you, Muriel."

"I bet it was Bloop," said Muriel. "She always was a little stinker."

Rory was about to confess, when the coach pulled into the zoo. Over the noise of the excited children, the penguins could hear the familiar roaring of tigers and smell the comforting, earthy aroma of the elephants.

"Home sweet home," sighed Blue as the driver wheeled the cello case down the ramp and parked it. He called a cheery goodbye to Mrs Slingsby and, promising to return after the carol concert to pick up the children, he left.

"Where are we?" said Blue.

Rory lifted the lid slightly and looked

out. "By Santa's Grotto," he said. "Let's get out while no one's looking and mingle."

Standing in their disguises in the shadows, lit by soft, flickering candlelight, it was hard to distinguish the penguins from the infants. As Blue looked around at the sight before them, her eyes grew wider and wider.

"Are you sure this is our zoo, Rory?"

Since they'd left in the sleigh, the grounds of City Zoo had been transformed – they looked like a scene from a Victorian Christmas card. There were stalls selling mulled wine, hot mince pies and chestnuts. There was a carousel lit up with hundreds of coloured lights and, as it went round, brightly painted horses gave rides to the children.

MINCE
PIES

"Can we just have *one* go," pleaded Blue, "before we go back to our hutches?"

"Why not?" said Rory. "We couldn't get into any more trouble if we tried."

The horses were on poles, too high for the penguins to reach, but luckily the man in charge of the rides mistook them for toddlers and lifted them on, two to a horse.

"You hardly weigh a feather, love," he said, lifting Blue on to a piebald pony; he picked Rory up and put him in the same saddle.

"Room for another little'un," he said. "Hold on tight, you two!"

Blue put her flippers round Rory's waist. As the organ music started up, the carousel began to spin and, as the horses went up and down, they had an amazing view of the zoo.

"Look, Rory, there're the chimpanzees… they're waving! And there's the giraffe… and the lions!"

"Oh, and there's the penguin pool again!" said Rory as they went round for the tenth time.

"Time to go home," said Blue.

The organ music stopped and the man who ran the ride helped them off. "Merry Christmas!" he said. "I hope you get everything you wished for."

Rory and Blue held flippers and ran over to the wall of their enclosure.

"What did you wish for, Blue?" asked Rory.

"It's already come true," she said. "We're back where we belong."

Muriel, Hatty and Brenda were there, eating toffee apples.

"OK. Let's form a pyramid and get back over," said Rory.

"*Eugh!* Hatty and Brenda have sticky mittens!" squeaked Muriel as she climbed on to their shoulders. "Let's hope Santa brings them some new ones."

Blue balanced on top of Muriel, then Rory climbed up the penguin pyramid they had made, hopped on to the wall and pulled them all up.

"Uh-oh, I can see Paulie," he sighed. "He'll be furious with us for leaving the zoo."

One by one the penguins jumped down into their enclosure and, as Paulie approached, they bowed their heads and waited to be told off.

"What time do you call this?" he frowned.

"D-don't know," they mumbled.

"*You don't know?*" he boomed. "Then let me remind you. It's *Christmas* time!" To their surprise, Paulie's beak split into a huge smile.

"'Tis the season of goodwill to all penguins," he announced. "Yes, even the naughty ones."

As he gave them all a welcome-home hug, the sweet sound of music drifted towards them. Paulie cocked his head, put his flipper to his ear and listened.

"*Hark!*" he said. "*The Herald Angels Sing!*"

The carol service had begun. Full of Christmas spirit, Paulie's voice rang out and the penguins, the rhinos, the gorillas and all the animals from the gerbils to the giraffe joined in with the singing. *Ding Dong Merrily on High.*

"Marvellous orchestra," Paulie said afterwards. "Pity there was no cello."

But Charlotte Higginbottom didn't miss it one bit.

CHAPTER TEN

The First Noel

It was the night before Christmas and, remembering all the wonderful things they'd learnt about it at school, the penguins couldn't wait to see what tomorrow would bring.

"Nothing," said Orson. "Penguins don't

celebrate Christmas."

"Only bears do," said Ursie, waving a Wellington. "Excuse me while I hang up my boot. Santa puts something in it every year because I'm such good bear, aren't I, Orson?"

Orson shook his head, then punched him playfully. "You're a very bad bear, but hey, that's why I like you!"

Rory felt a bit jealous. It didn't seem fair that Santa only gave presents to the bears, but maybe they were making it up. They were famous for spreading rumours that were completely untrue, so he decided to double-check.

"Ursie, how do you know it's Santa and not Orson who gives you presents?"

Ursie flapped his paw as if the answer was obvious. "I've seen him, of course. I stay awake all night every Christmas Eve."

Rory hadn't finished quizzing him. "What does Santa look like then?"

"Oh, you know… kind of brown and furry."

Rory smiled to himself. Santa didn't look anything like that, but as it was Christmas, it would have been mean to point it out.

"Come on, Blue," he said softly, "I'm not sure if Santa visits City Zoo for real."

Muriel, however, overheard him. "He does, Rory!" she said, stamping her foot. "Hatty and Brenda, tell Rory and Bloop that Santa *is* going to come."

"Ho ho," said Hatty flatly.

"Ho!" added Brenda.

Muriel undid the drawstring on her precious PE bag and rummaged about inside. "Right! If you don't believe me, I'll prove it," she said, pulling out a football sock and giving it to Rory.

"Hang that up at the end of your nest," she said, "and when you wake and it's got a present in, you'll know Santa's been. Here's one for you, Bloop."

Muriel gave her a little cotton ankle sock. Blue held it up and laughed – it wouldn't hold many presents.

Paulie, who had been watching and listening, offered some words of wisdom. "Sometimes the best things come in small packages, Blue."

"And some come in *extra large*," said Muriel, helping herself to the longest sock in the bag. "Hatty and Brenda, here are yours. Don't say I never give you anything."

Unfortunately there weren't enough of Muriel's socks for every penguin in the pool, but thankfully Waldo had a stash of lost property in his hutch and, when he got wind of the stocking shortage, he sorted everyone out with something.

"Will Santa mind if I hang up this ladies' handbag instead of a stocking?" wondered Alaskadabra, the old emperor penguin.

"He'll have to put up with it, love," said Waldo. "I'm not made of socks."

One by one, the penguins drifted back to their hutches, clutching various hats, gloves and bootees in the hope that Santa would come and fill them with gifts. All except for Paulie. Waldo had offered him the leg from a pair of woolly tights, but he refused to take it.

"Thanks, but no, thanks. I'm a penguin. Christmas is not for me."

Rory walked Blue back to her hutch. "Maybe Santa will come after all," he said excitedly.

Blue gave his flipper a squeeze. "Don't get your hopes up. Remember what Paulie said."

But that Christmas Eve as Rory slept, something disturbed him at midnight. Was it the sound of sleigh bells? Half awake, he swore he heard footsteps and saw a stout figure in red, with a long white beard, at the end of his nest. He rubbed his eyes, but there was no one there; he must have been dreaming. He sighed and went back to sleep.

*

Just before dawn, Rory was woken by a loud hammering on the door – it was Blue. She held her ankle sock up to the window. "Rory, wake up! Santa's been!"

He sat up and felt the toe of his sock. There was a bulge in it – he could hardly believe it.

Blue came in and sat in his nest. "Let's open our stockings together."

There was a parcel in each sock. Blue ripped off the paper with her beak: Santa had given her a hairslide covered in diamonds.

"Oh, it's lovely!" she cried, clipping it into her feathers. "What did he get you, Rory?"

It was a set of sparkly wheels for his skateboard.

"Cool! How did Santa know I needed new ones?"

"He knows if we've been bad or good," said Blue. "He knows everything."

Rory was amazed. Muriel had got it right for once – Santa did visit the zoo!

"Yeah, but just in case he didn't, I got you this," said Blue, handing him a present.

To her surprise, he felt under his nest and gave her a small package as well.

"Me too, Blue."

"You go first," she said.

Rory undid the tissue paper. It was the glass polar bear from the school Christmas tree.

"I will treasure it forever," he murmured.

"I know how much you miss Frosty," said Blue, undoing her gift from him.

"Hope you like it," said Rory.

It was the little bracelet made from elastic and beads from one of the Christmas crackers.

"Like it?" said Blue. "I *love* it... it's a necklace, right?"

It wasn't, but that was just as well because penguins don't have wrists and, as Rory slipped it over Blue's head, he was glad he'd chosen it – it fitted perfectly.

"Happy Christmas, Squiddo," he said. "Shall we go and see what the others got?"

They raced outside and almost fell over backwards when they saw the penguin enclosure – it was sparkling with bright paper chains, baubles and tinsel. Someone had even hung a piece of mistletoe from the diving board.

"All our own work," said Waldo proudly, putting his flippers round Wesley and Warren. "We've been up half the night, haven't we, boys?"

They weren't the only ones. Ursie and Orson had waited up for Santa and they weren't disappointed – he appeared to have brought them matching gold medallions.

"They're solid gold," said Ursie.

"They're solid chocolate," corrected Orson. "By the way, thanks for the Christmas card, you guys. We loved it. We didn't know penguins celebrated Christmas."

"But we do now, don't we, Orson?" said Ursie. "So, next year, we'll send them a card. Ooh, *someone* must have been a very good girl!"

Muriel arrived. She came waddling over wearing a ladies' fascinator on her head made from pink feathers, a pair of diamond clip-on earrings attached to her flippers and a pearl necklace slung round her waist like a belt.

"Santa gave me this!" she boasted. "And Brenda gave me this, and Hatty gave me—" Suddenly she spotted Warren and went all coy. "Did you get my Christmas card, Warren?" she simpered, standing under the mistletoe. Warren nodded, twirled his moustache and blushed.

"I have put it on my wall. You're a fine artist, Muriel."

Muriel whirled her pearls with glee and blew him a string of kisses.

"Hear that? *Warren* knows a good artist when he sees one!" she said, glaring at Hatty and Brenda. "*He* recognised my painting for what it was straight away, unlike certain penguins I can mention."

"It was the best portrait of a hippo I have ever seen," said Warren sincerely.

Ignoring Hatty and Brenda's giggles,

Muriel gave him her warmest smile. "I knew hippos were your favourite mammal, Warren. That's why I painted one for you – didn't I say I was painting a lovely hippo for Warren, Hatty and Brenda?"

"We *all* said it was a lovely hippo," said Hatty, "because that's what it looks like."

"Because you're so good at painting," added Brenda.

Then the emperor chicks arrived with Big Paulie, who was still in his red dressing gown. They had woken him up at three in the morning and were falling over themselves with excitement.

"Unky Pooey, you will *never* geth what Thanta gave me!" said Oo-Chi, shooting her beloved uncle with a spud gun loaded with sprats' eyes.

"And Unky Pooey," said Ku-Chi, blowing his new toy trumpet as loudly as he could in Paulie's ear, "you will *never* not even geth what Thanta gave *me*!"

Paulie rolled his eyes. He tugged at the little bit of white, fluffy cotton wool that had somehow got itself stuck to his chin and puffed it away.

"There are times," he said, "when I really wish Santa didn't exist!"

"Did he bring you a present?" asked Rory.

For a moment, Paulie didn't answer. He felt the little glass penguin in his pocket that someone had left on the front step of the palace and, as his beloved penguins gathered round him, he smiled.

"Rory, Santa gave me the best present ever – Christmas with my friends and family."

And after that, no one celebrated
Christmas more joyfully than the penguins
at City Zoo.

Read the first hilarious penguin story!

Rory and his penguin pals are in a panic!

Their zoo might have to close if more people
don't come to visit. So when the zookeeper
installs PENGUIN CAM, the determined birds
decide to put on a talent show starring a very
daring stunt team.

Will the penguins' performance save the zoo or
will it just be pandemonium?

Awe**s**ome **Animals**

Awes**ome adventures
with the **wildest** wildlife!**

Meerkat Madness — IAN WHYBROW

More Meerkat Madness — IAN WHYBROW

Meerkat Madness Flying High — IAN WHYBROW

Merry Meerkat Madness — IAN WHYBROW

Watch out for the world's wildest pandas!

PANDA PANIC — Jamie Rix

PANDA PANIC Running Wild — Jamie Rix

Penguin Pandemonium Little birds, big dreams — Jeanne Willis

Penguin Pandemonium The Rescue

Penguin Pandemonium The Wild Beast — Jeanne Willis

Go to
www.awesomeanimalsbooks.com
for awesome videos
and competitions